THE
WEREWOLF
OF WARWICK

by Anne Schraff

Perfection Learning® Corporation
Logan, Iowa 51546

Cover Design: Mark Hagenberg

Cover Image Credit: Cathy McKinty/Acclaim Images
(image modifications by Mike Aspengren)

For information, contact:
Perfection Learning® Corporation
1000 North Second Avenue, P.O. Box 500,
Logan, Iowa 51546-0500.
Phone: 1-800-831-4190 • Fax: 1-800-543-2745
perfectionlearning.com

PB ISBN-13: 978-0-7891-6667-8 ISBN-10:0-7891-6667-4
RLB ISBN-13: 978-0-7569-4766-8   ISBN-10: 0-7569-4766-9

9 10 11 12 13 PP 23 22 21 20 19

1 "IT'S A WEREWOLF!" screamed 17-year-old Mallorie McIntyre. Then she broke into a grin. Brendon Hayes was standing before her in full makeup, including bushy eyebrows, pointy ears, hairy palms, and long fingernails.

Brendon was the star at a small local theater in *The Werewolf of Warwick*, a musical spoof of the werewolf legends. The play was written and directed by Paul Axton. Most of the cast consisted of college students, but Mallorie and a few others were seniors at Kennedy High School. Mallorie had been working at the theater taking tickets, but to her huge delight, this time she got a tiny part in the play. She was to be one of the frightened townspeople of Warwick who ran through the shadowed night with the werewolf in hot pursuit.

Mallorie had performed in several plays in high school, and she dreamed of becoming an actress. She loved everything about the theater—the make-believe, the lighting, the costumes, and most of all, the excitement of performing before a live audience.

"So you like my gory makeup, huh?" Brendon laughed. He was very handsome but a little bit stuck on himself. From the first moment Mallorie saw Brendon, she'd had a crush on him, but she knew she didn't have a chance. Brendon was already dating another girl, Vicky Adams. Vicky was a tall, beautiful girl who was playing the female lead in the play, Lady Cordelia. Mallorie always watched enviously as the pair sang their duets in each other's arms.

Brendon playfully lifted his clawlike hands and grabbed for Mallorie. "Come to me, my pretty," he said in his deep werewolf voice. "I want to munch on you for lunch!" Brendon's furry hands closed on Mallorie's wrist, and she squealed in mock fear.

"Okay, okay, you guys, let's stop the horsing around and get busy. We've got a lot of rehearsing to do, and Mr. Axton just pulled up," Cole Whitman said. Though he was also only a senior at Kennedy High, Cole was coordinating the play. He was a genius with sound, lighting, and organization. He was tall and thin with owlish glasses that Mallorie thought made him look pretty nerdy. But he commanded a lot of respect around the theater because of his competence. He had asked Mallorie out once or twice, but she always turned him down. He just wasn't her type.

Vicky flounced down the stage in her black-velvet-trimmed purple period dress and smiled at Mallorie. "Do I look adorable or what? I'll have you know I made this dress with my own hands just so it would be perfect!" she said.

"It looks great, Vicky," Mallorie said. Mallorie thought ruefully that with Vicky around, Brendon probably couldn't even see other girls.

As they prepared for a scene, Vicky launched into one of her extravagant stories she was always telling. She was chronically dramatic—not just when she was acting. "Do you know about the curse of the Sierra Theater, Mallorie?" she asked.

"No," Mallorie said. Her family had just moved into the neighborhood last year, so she didn't know much about its history.

"Mr. Axton and I are pretty close, and he confides in me a lot," Vicky said in a confidential voice. "Turns out this used to be a movie theater, and then they closed it down and tried to stage plays here. Well, there was a horrible murder right here in the theater about 20 years ago. This crazed, lovesick guy hurled his girlfriend from the balcony—right up there where the green curtains are now—and she died of a broken neck right where we are standing!"

Mallorie had worked for Mr. Axton for nearly a year. She couldn't imagine the serious, passionate 45-year-old man confiding in Vicky. "Are you sure about that, Vicky? I mean, it's not one of those silly urban legends people tell, is it?" Mallorie said.

Vicky looked offended. "Mallorie! How dare you call me a liar! I wouldn't have told you if it wasn't true. And I haven't even told you the worst part yet. The murderer sprinted down the stairs and fled the theater into the dark night and was never seen again. He was never brought to justice, so he's probably still lurking around here!" Vicky finished the tale with a dramatic flourish.

"That's awful," Mallorie said, not sure if she believed it or not.

"And you know what else?" Vicky said in a lowered voice. "For 20 years, the theater was locked up because of what happened. And sometimes people walking by on the street heard this strange voice howling from inside the theater, calling out 'Cassandra . . . Cassandra' like it was the murderer calling to the girl he had killed. Her name was Cassandra . . ."

Mallorie just nodded. Vicky was pretty emotional. She was known to embellish the truth, to make whatever she was talking about more dramatic or exciting. She often tossed the names of famous people around, and she would claim she and her family had been dining at some restaurant when a celebrity came in and chatted with them. Vicky's parents were wealthy, and they often went to check on their properties in Hollywood, Brentwood, and Beverly Hills, so Mallorie thought it was possible that they ran into movie and television stars. But she doubted it.

"Well, the theater is all bright and painted now," Mallorie said cheerfully, "so if there was a ghost hanging around, it's probably taken a hike."

Vicky looked angry. When she told her stories, she expected the listener to be properly impressed and amazed. Mallorie was making a joke out of it, and she could tell Vicky was furious.

Mr. Axton came striding into the theater, his customary frown making creases in his weary face. Mallorie heard that he had once dreamed of writing and directing major Broadway plays, but the tide had always gone against him. Now he was grumpily content to do theater in medium-sized cities.

"We need to rehearse the scene where the young townswoman gets attacked by the werewolf as she is hurrying from her kitchen-maid job late at night," Mr. Axton said. He looked around until he saw Mallorie. "There you are. You know how the scene goes. It's a small scene, but it sets the stage for the theme of terror, so it's pivotal."

Mallorie was so excited to be a part of the play. She had hunted the costume shops around town looking for just the right costume. Now she was dressed as a kitchen maid of the 18th century. All the actors had to provide their own costumes because the theater had a very low budget.

Mallorie emerged from the doorway and paled under the flickering glow of a streetlamp. Gas lamps lit the little 18th-century village. Mallorie glanced around nervously.

"No, no, no," Mr. Axton shouted. "You are already looking frightened, Mallorie, and you have no idea yet that the werewolf is stalking you! You must show weariness, not fear! You are coming home after a hard day's work, and all you can think of is a night of rest from your labors. Your attitude must be one of weariness."

Mallorie changed her expression to indifference and walked with the stooped shoulders of a weary worker. She ran her hand over her brow as if trying to wipe away the day's toil, and she sang her little ditty. "Alas I work from sun to sun! A servant's work is never done!"

"Good! Good!" Mr. Axton shouted. "And there is a lovely timbre to your voice, Mallorie. I had not noticed that before."

Mallorie walked slowly across the stage. A dark shadow, illuminated by the streetlamp, appeared behind her. But Mallorie was oblivious to it. She remembered the instructions. She did not yet know the danger she was in.

A figure clad in black had begun following her. A dark scarf obscured his face, but as he closed in on the girl, he reached out with a clawed hand and touched her.

Mallorie turned. She was staring into the horrific face of the wolfman, the dreaded werewolf. Mallorie clasped her hands to her cheeks and began to run.

The creature followed her, grasping for her and soon overtaking her. Even though it was just a play, Mallorie really managed to feel the stark horror of being swallowed up in the arms of the monstrous creature whose face was covered in bristly hair. For a few seconds she was so lost in the play that Brendon terrified her.

Mallorie swooned, and the werewolf swiftly gathered her in his arms, running offstage with the helpless, unconscious girl, her arms dangling at her sides.

"Perfect!" Mr. Axton shouted. "An outstanding job, Mallorie and Brendon!"

Offstage, Brendon put Mallorie down gently. He smiled at her. "We're good," he said. "We are very good. I am so excited, I could bite you!"

But instead of biting Mallorie, Brendon planted an impulsive kiss on her cheek.

Mallorie almost swooned again, this time for real.

Brendon had kissed her!

In her fantasies it had happened several times, but she never thought it would happen in real life. Even though Brendon was covered with his hideous makeup, the experience overwhelmed her. Brendon had kissed her! She kept repeating that fact over and over to herself. She kept saying, "Oh wow, oh wow, oh wow."

Mallorie didn't notice the other girl standing offstage waiting for her cue. There was a look of hurt and shock on Vicky's face. Her lower lip was trembling, and she was on the verge of tears.

"Vicky!" Mr. Axton called her on stage. "You are engaged to young John Winston, the unfortunate young man who occasionally turns into the werewolf. You have no idea the young man is so grievously afflicted, but your love for him is so great that as the horror unfolds, you will accept him unconditionally. Now, you sit before your dressing table mirror in a rhapsody of love, thinking of your beloved."

Vicky sat before the mirror in her beautiful purple dress and began to sing. "I am lucky. I am fortunate. I am to be a bride; John Winston is my darling, whom I shall walk beside."

"Vicky," Mr. Axton cried, "that is so blah! You sound bored. You must do it with feeling! You are in love, charged with emotion. Again!"

Vicky looked nervous. She had a beautiful voice, but now she sang in a monotone.

"I am lucky. I am fortunate," she began again.

"Stop!" Mr. Axton shouted. "Is there another girl here with a good singing voice who could show Vicky how to put more life into the song? You, Mallorie, can you sing with spirit and show Vicky how it's done?"

Mallorie didn't know what possessed her to be so bold as to agree to perform the scene. She walked on stage in her maid outfit and positioned herself before the mirror. She reached up to primp her hair as she sang.

"I am lucky," she belted with flair, "I am fortunate! I am to be a bride! John Winston is my dar—ling, whom I shall walk beside!"

Mr. Axton applauded vigorously. "That's the way. That's the idea. Did you see how Mallorie did it, Vicky? That's what I'm looking for. Did you notice her showmanship, the twinkle, the flair? Remember, dear girl, this is not some heavy, dreary drama. It's a spoof. We must keep before the audience the delicious contrast between horror and fun. The lyrics are meant to be lighthearted and silly. There is fun in Mallorie's voice!" he said.

Mallorie caught the expression on Vicky's face. It gave fresh meaning to the phrase "if looks could kill." Vicky looked as if she would have enjoyed the opportunity to strangle Mallorie. But Mallorie hadn't shown her up on purpose. It had just happened.

Vicky tried the song again, and it was even worse than the earlier tries. Now she was so nervous, she was fouling it up completely. Mr. Axton told her to practice at home, and they'd try again tomorrow. Then he went on to other scenes.

When the rehearsal finally ended at 9:30, and the cast was filing out, Vicky caught up to Mallorie. "That was the cruelest thing I ever saw, Mallorie McIntyre," she said in a bitter voice.

"Vicky! What did I do?" Mallorie protested. "Mr. Axton asked me to do the song to help you get it right. That's all I was doing. I wanted to help you get it right."

"You don't fool me for a moment, you deceiving little witch," Vicky cried. "I'm a theater major, and this role means a lot to me. You're just a little high school loser. Don't you dare ever try to upstage me again, or you'll be sorry!"

Mallorie was shocked by the hatred on Vicky's face. In some way it made her uglier than Brendon with all his horrific makeup.

It was like looking at pure evil.

2 MALLORIE LIVED RIGHT OFF the bus line, about three miles from the theater. So after rehearsal, she always walked three blocks and took the bus home. Now as she walked the three blocks to the bus stop in the darkness, she was aware of how spooky everything looked at night. During the day, most of the businesses were open, and the sidewalk was bustling with people. Now everything was closed, and the shadows falling from the buildings made Mallorie cringe.

Maybe it was the nature of the play that was making her uneasy. Or maybe she was still shaken from Vicky's outburst. Whatever it was, Mallorie felt nervous.

Right after high school graduation in June, Mallorie planned to buy a car. She would have enough of her own money saved by then to buy a nice used one. Her mom and dad had offered to help her buy a car sooner, but it was a matter of principle with Mallorie. She wanted to use the money she had been saving since she was 13.

She wished she were riding in a car right now instead of walking. Most of the stores Mallorie passed had been closed since 7:00. She kept recalling the stalking scene in the play where the werewolf ends up grabbing the girl.

"I'm just being silly," Mallorie scolded herself.

At the corner up ahead stood a man in a dark pullover sweater and dark jeans. He was smoking a cigarette. Mallorie saw the tiny light of his cigarette burning in the darkness. He was probably just a guy taking a break on his way home from work, she thought.

Or maybe not. He looked a little shady. He had bushy eyebrows that seemed to meet in the middle of his forehead.

This is just stupid, Mallorie told herself. Stop being a chicken and grow up!

The man didn't even look at Mallorie as she passed him. But when she was a few steps away from him, he called out in a strange, slurred voice, "You got any change for a cup of coffee?"

Mallorie was startled. And scared. "Uh . . ." she mumbled, fishing in her purse. She found three quarters and hastily gave them to the man.

"Thank you," he muttered, walking away down a side street. He probably didn't want coffee, she thought. He probably wanted another pack of cigarettes.

Finally Mallorie got to the bus stop. She breathed a sigh of relief as she waited for the bus and winced at the shadows a nearby tree made. Mallorie had worked at the theater for nearly a year already, taking tickets for the plays they had. Going home at night like this had never bothered her before.

But this was the first time she was part of a play about a werewolf. The scene she had rehearsed earlier was freaking her out now.

Mallorie smiled and shook her head.

Get real, will you? she told herself. There are no such things as werewolves. This is a nice, peaceful neighborhood, and nobody has to be afraid of walking to the bus stop before 10:00 at night!

Mallorie tried to take her mind off

her uneasiness, so she thought about Brendon's kiss. Brendon was the best-looking, most interesting boy Mallorie had ever seen. There was not a single guy at Kennedy High School who made her feel the way Brendon did. He was only 19, a sophomore at the college. He wasn't that much older than Mallorie. But Mallorie knew they could be friends and that was about it. Vicky always bragged that she and Brendon were all either of them ever needed. She called Brendon "my sweet guy."

It was ridiculous for Mallorie to think anything could happen between her and Brendon.

"Where's that bus?" Mallorie muttered to herself. In a few minutes, it would be 10:00. The bus was late.

Mallorie wondered if the murder story Vicky had told her about the girl named Cassandra was true. Mallorie supposed some lovesick guy could have followed his faithless girlfriend into the theater and thrown her from the balcony. People did crazy things when they were in love. Look at Shakespeare's plays. Poor Romeo took poison, and Juliet stabbed herself. That was pretty crazy. As crazy as pushing your girlfriend off a balcony and breaking her neck.

Mallorie shuddered as she thought that if, by some incredible turn of events, Brendon fell in love with Mallorie and dropped Vicky, Vicky would probably push Mallorie off the balcony at the Sierra Theater. Or try to!

Mallorie turned her thoughts to Mr. Axton—Paul Vincent Axton. He seemed like a man who had an unhappy life. He was a nice-looking, middle-aged man who probably had been very handsome in his youth. It was sad to think that his dreams had never come true and that now he had resigned himself to second best. But he was still working in the theater, which he obviously loved, so that was good.

Mallorie wondered if Mr. Axton had known the young lovers who had the fight on the balcony that night. She wondered if he had seen the fatal plunge. If it really happened, that is.

The bus appeared then, and Mallorie climbed on. Nobody else from the play took the bus home. Most of them either had their own cars or carpooled. When they first started rehearsing for the werewolf play, Cole had offered to drive Mallorie home, but she turned him down because she didn't want to give him hope that she liked him. Once she started accepting favors from him, he might think she would agree to go out with him.

"You're late, Mallorie," Mrs. McIntyre said when she got home. Mallorie's parents were in the kitchen making cookies. They both had demanding jobs, and when they were home, they loved to do things together, like make cookies for the church bake sale.

"Yeah, we were getting concerned," Mallorie's dad said. "Maybe when rehearsals are late like this, I could come pick you up. I'm not too thrilled about you coming down that dark street to the bus stop, honey."

Mallorie didn't want her father coming to pick her up. It would be embarrassing. Anyway, he worked hard all day, and he deserved his evenings free of being a taxi service. "Thanks, Dad, but I like riding the bus," Mallorie said.

"But it's dark, and you're a young girl walking alone. Most of the businesses are shut down for the night," Mr. McIntyre said. "I'd just feel better coming to get you."

"Cole Whitman said he'd drive me home," Mallorie said quickly. Riding with Cole would be better than involving her father.

"Okay," he said. "That sounds good. Cole is a fine young man. I like him. His mom has that great bakery over on Union."

You would like him, Mallorie thought wryly. He's every father's dream date for his daughter—polite, nice, intelligent, hardworking. A guy who would never dream of sneaking up to a girl and kissing her, like Brendon did. A guy without an ounce of romantic daring. Cole was a piano-playing prodigy when he was six years old. Now he was president of the school chess team and member of the youth symphony.

But riding with Cole was now the only choice. Mallorie would just have to make sure he didn't get any ideas.

....

When Mallorie arrived at the theater for rehearsal the next day, only Mr. Axton was there.

"Mallorie," he said, "I know you come early, so I came extra early too in the hopes we'd have a few minutes alone to talk."

"What do you want to talk about, Mr. Axton?" she asked apprehensively.

"If Vicky does not show any improvement in her portrayal of Lady Cordelia, she will have to be replaced," he said bluntly. "The play hangs on Winston and Lady Cordelia. If either of those roles are poor, then the play will flop."

Mallorie gasped. "But taking that role away from Vicky? Are you kidding me?"

Mr. Axton didn't smile. He rarely did. "I do not joke about such serious matters. I must tell you that I was very taken with your singing yesterday. You are far superior to Vicky in style and substance. And you have spirit. I cannot imagine when we had open auditions why you didn't try out for Lady Cordelia. If it's best to replace Vicky, I'll give her another good role, but not the lead. Lady Cordelia is too important. Brendon is a superb John Winston, but a lackluster Cordelia makes even John look bad. What would you think about taking the role, Mallorie?" he asked.

"Oh, Mr. Axton! Vicky would be devastated," Mallorie groaned.

"But we have to think of the good of the play before the feelings of any one person. If the play is a flop, it will also reflect badly on her," Mr. Axton said. "If the reviewers tear apart our wimpy Cordelia, how will that be for her?"

"Maybe she'll be much better today, Mr. Axton," Mallorie said. But the idea of playing Cordelia was immensely appealing to Mallorie. She would have two marvelous love scenes with Brendon! It would give the two of them the chance to really get to know each other.

How can you even be thinking like that? A righteous little voice demanded inside Mallorie's head. He belongs to Vicky! He's Vicky's sweet guy.

Mr. Axton looked levelly at Mallorie and asked, "If I decide that Vicky is not able to continue in the role, may I depend upon you to take it?"

Mallorie nodded. "Yes. I think I could do a good job," she said, stunning herself by her words.

"I think so too," Mr. Axton said with just the trace of a smile.

Mallorie dreaded Vicky coming in. Part of Mallorie wanted Vicky to be so improved that she would wow Mr. Axton and keep her role. But another part of her wanted desperately to be Lady Cordelia and was hoping Vicky fell flat on her face, as cruel as that was.

Mallorie didn't want Vicky to be mad at her, and she knew Vicky would be furious if Mallorie took the role away from her. But even stronger was Mallorie's desire to really shine on that stage in the lead role.

When the rehearsal was under way, Mr. Axton put Vicky before the mirror and ordered her to launch into the scene that had been her undoing twice before.

"Have you practiced?" Mr. Axton demanded of her.

"Yes, oh, yes," Vicky said. "I know I'm much better now."

Mallorie couldn't bear to look at her. She was trying too hard. Mallorie felt so sorry for her. It must be awful to be on the spot like that, Mallorie thought.

But still, in her heart, Mallorie was drooling with anticipation. She was so close to the dream role of Lady Cordelia.

"I know I've fixed the problem I had before," Vicky said. She looked like she was about to cry rather than sing.

Vicky launched into the scene, and, if anything, she was worse than before. Now she was nervous in addition to being flat and dull.

In an almost-gentle voice, Mr. Axton told Vicky to go into his office and wait for him. Then he talked to Brendon for a few minutes. Finally he went into the office and closed the door.

After about 15 minutes, Vicky emerged, her eyes red from crying. She ran to a friend, Laura, and fell into her arms, sobbing. Mallorie overheard some of the words Vicky said. "Axton is taking Cordelia away from me! I have to play Hortense, the stupid boardinghouse woman!"

Laura tried to comfort Vicky, but Vicky broke away from her embrace and walked over to where Mallorie stood in silence. Vicky stood there glaring at Mallorie. Vicky was silent but her lips formed a clear message.

"You'll pay for this!"

3 LOOKING AT VICKY, Mallorie felt terrible, but then she told herself it simply wasn't her fault that any of this happened. Mr. Axton had picked her for Lady Cordelia because Vicky wasn't doing a good job. It wasn't like Mallorie had undermined Vicky or campaigned for the role.

Mallorie wondered how bad Brendon would feel now that his girlfriend had lost the female lead opposite him. Maybe he'd be so disappointed that it would affect his performance too. But when Brendon got up to do his scene, he seemed fine. Mallorie had never seen him perform this well.

"I am a werewolf, through no fault of mine!" Brendon sang in his rich tenor voice. "Believe me, I would rather be a creature more benign!"

"Splendid," Mr. Axton said. "You have captured just the right tone, Brendon."

Mallorie turned away from Vicky sulking over in the corner. She was becoming familiar with her new role as the boardinghouse lady. All Hortense, her new character, had to do was look frazzled and frumpy, whine, and sing one common refrain: "I cannot understand why there's so much hair. In the corners, on the floor, your room is like a lair! Mr. Winston, you must be the hairiest man I ever did see!"

Mallorie joined Brendon then for one of their scenes together, and because Mallorie hadn't had time to learn the lines, she just followed Brendon's lead and did the gestures.

At the end of the rehearsal day, Mr. Axton called Mallorie aside. "You must study very hard to learn your part. We haven't got much time. But you are a very bright young lady, and I know you can do it," he said.

"I will. I am sure of it," Mallorie promised, clutching the playbook.

Mallorie remembered then the story Vicky had told about the murder 20 years ago. She decided to indulge her curiosity. "Mr. Axton, somebody told me that a murder happened here a long time ago, and that's why the theater was closed for such a long time. A guy supposedly pushed his girlfriend off the balcony and killed her and then ran off," Mallorie said.

Mr. Axton's face became immediately disfigured with shock and rage. "Who told you such a preposterous story?" he demanded.

"Uh, well, somebody . . . I don't remember," Mallorie said, not wanting to get Vicky into trouble.

"Well, that person is lying! The person who told you that is a falsifier who doesn't deserve any attention for those outrageous stories!" Mr. Axton intoned angrily. "Nothing of the sort happened in this theater. A murder, indeed! Never! Of all the ridiculous, absurd nonsense. Mallorie, don't spread this to another person. A horrible rumor like that could do damage to our revitalized theater, to our dreams of a season of plays. Do you understand?"

"Yes, Mr. Axton. I won't say a word about it," Mallorie promised.

"Good girl," Mr. Axton said, taking

Mallorie's hand and patting it. He seemed to calm down slightly. "I knew you were a very sensible girl the moment I met you. I wish I had known how talented you were. We would not have wasted our time with Vicky. You have a lovely, stirring voice and a very beautiful face. You will make a splendid Lady Cordelia!"

Mallorie walked from the theater with confused emotions. She had been so surprised and bewildered by the dramatic events of the evening that she'd forgotten to ask Cole for a ride home. So she was stuck taking the bus again.

Mallorie wondered why the story of the murder at the theater had driven Mr. Axton into such a frenzy of denial. Was there some truth to it? Otherwise, why had he reacted so violently? Mallorie was sure now that Vicky had not heard the story from Mr. Axton. He never would have confided in anyone about something that could harm the production of his plays. She obviously had another source.

Something bad, something tragic had happened at the Sierra Theater 20 years ago. Mallorie was pretty sure of that. It had stood boarded up for so long according to Kelly Sloan, Mallorie's best friend. There were many attempts to open it as a warehouse, an auction house, and then a playhouse, but something always stood in the way. Kelly's family had lived in the neighborhood for a long time. Mallorie decided to ask her for more information at school tomorrow.

Mallorie started down the street toward the bus stop. She became nervous again walking past all the closed stores. There were dark corners and shadows. She wished she had remembered to ask Cole for a ride.

As Mallorie passed a closed discount store, she saw the man in the dark clothing who had frightened her yesterday. There he was, in the middle of the sidewalk. He had given her the creeps before, and now she didn't even have any money to give him if he asked. Mallorie had spent her last change on a snack during rehearsal.

Mallorie looked around for some alternate route to follow so she wouldn't have to meet the man on the sidewalk. She noticed a little walkway alongside a closed hardware store leading back to an alley. Maybe, she thought, she could go down to the alley and cut around the block, avoiding the shady man.

Mallorie turned and started down the walkway. It was extremely dark and definitely scary. Battered aluminum garbage cans stood at angles. When Mallorie got to the alley, she turned and hurried along. She was eager to get to the end of the alley and then to cut back to the main drag, beyond where the man was standing.

Suddenly Mallorie got the terrible feeling that someone was following her. She heard a noise behind her, like someone clearing his throat. Mallorie was afraid to look back, scared it would be him and she would freak out. But Mallorie forced herself to look back over her shoulder. She saw a figure coming, gaining on her!

"Oh no, oh no, oh no," Mallorie groaned, breaking into a run. She had to get back to the street where that gas station on the corner was open. She couldn't let him catch her back here with nobody around!

Maybe he just wanted some change to go buy cigarettes. Or maybe not. Maybe he was just one of those aggressive beggars that seemed to be everywhere these days. Or maybe he was dangerous . . .

Mallorie looked back again. He was still coming.

"Girl," the man called to her.

Mallorie felt like running faster, but it was no use—she could not outrun him. So Mallorie turned toward him and shouted in a strong voice, "What do you want? My dad is just around the corner there. What do you want? Do you want to talk to my dad?"

"You got change for a cup of coffee?" the man asked.

"No. I have no money. I'm sorry," Mallorie said. "I see my dad now. I have to go."

The man stopped and stared after Mallorie with a blank look. Mallorie again noticed the strange way his eyebrows wandered over the bridge of his nose. She shook her head. She was definitely freaked out because of the play.

Mallorie hurried on, her heart beating

faster. She was running when she reached the main street and could breathe a sigh of relief. The final block she had to walk housed the open gas station and a bar that was open all night. It had blue and yellow neon signs in the window, blinking on and off. It had looked lurid to Mallorie before, but now it looked comforting. Mallorie felt safer. If the man followed her here, at least there was somewhere to go for help.

But he didn't seem to be following her anymore.

When Mallorie got to the bus stop, she was still breathing hard, but she tried to calm herself. What's the matter with you? she asked herself. Some poor, harmless beggar asks you for some change, and you're acting like you've been attacked. Okay, so he looks a little bit like a werewolf, but he's not one. That's your imagination working overtime.

The bus was due any minute. Mallorie felt much better.

And then she saw a white Subaru. Vicky's white Subaru.

Mallorie was stunned. What was Vicky doing here?

"Hi, Mallorie," Vicky shouted out the window. "Listen, I'm sorry about how I acted tonight at the theater. I was a big crybaby, and I blamed you when you didn't do anything."

"That's okay," Mallorie said gratefully, happy that Vicky didn't retain any hard feelings after all. But it was a shock. It didn't seem like Vicky's nature to forgive and forget.

"I'll drive you home," Vicky offered.

"Oh, thanks," Mallorie said. The bus was now in view, and Mallorie stepped away from the bus stop and waved the driver on. He nodded and continued down the street.

Mallorie went to the passenger door of the Subaru and tried to open it. It was locked. Mallorie knocked on the window and signaled for Vicky to push the little lever on the door, springing the lock on Mallorie's side.

"That was the last bus tonight, wasn't it?" Vicky shouted.

"What?" Mallorie said, bewildered. Why did Vicky say that? Why wasn't she opening the car door?

A look appeared on Vicky's face that Mallorie had not seen before. It was beyond hate. It was a smile without warmth. It was the kind of smile you would see on the face of a crocodile while its jaws clamped down on its victim in the swamp waters. Vicky gunned the Subaru forward, almost knocking Mallorie into the brush along the road.

Vicky looked back once. She was laughing.

Mallorie stood there, shocked. Vicky had never intended to give Mallorie a ride home. She had only promised her a ride so that Mallorie would miss the last bus. Vicky wanted her to be stranded late at night in the middle of nowhere.

Mallorie was three miles from her home. It would take her 45 minutes to walk there. She'd be so late that her parents would be worried sick. Besides, part of the road she'd have to walk on was a two-lane highway where there wasn't even a sidewalk. She'd have to struggle along on the brushy shoulder of the road.

Mallorie had to go back to the business district. All she could do was pray that the gas station was still open so she could call for her dad to come get her.

Please let the gas station be open, she prayed.

4 MALLORIE RAN BACK down the street toward the gas station. It had been open 15 minutes earlier. But would it still be open now?

How could Vicky have done such a thing to me? Mallorie asked herself. It wasn't Mallorie's fault that Mr. Axton had replaced Vicky as Lady Cordelia. If Mallorie had refused the part, he would have gotten another girl. It just wasn't fair that Vicky was blaming her.

As Mallorie approached the gas station, she saw a middle-aged lady in the snack shop attached to the self-service pumps. Mallorie rushed in. "Ma'am," she said, "I need to make a phone call."

"We don't have a pay phone anymore," the woman said. She was munching on corn chips from an open bag. "Not enough people using it. Most folks have cells."

"Ma'am, you must have a phone in your office there. Could I please use that?" Mallorie asked.

"I'm sorry. We don't let our customers

use our private phone. It's a rule the boss has," the woman said.

"But it's an emergency," Mallorie said.

"I can call 911 for you," the woman said. "I can do that."

"No, it's just that I need to call my dad to come get me," Mallorie said.

"There's a bar down the street. They got a pay phone," the woman said. "Toddle on down there, missy."

Mallorie left the gas station and walked down to the bar. She glanced at the flashing neon "beer and wine" sign and entered the dark establishment.

"Do you have a pay phone?" Mallorie asked the bartender.

"Yes, over there, little lady," he said, pointing to a corner.

Some men sitting on stools along the bar started chuckling. Mallorie figured they were speculating on why a nearly hysterical teenager was out at this hour. Mallorie reached the pay phone and then remembered that she had no money. She ran back to the bartender. "Mister, I don't have any change for the phone," Mallorie pleaded, her voice trailing off.

The bartender handed her some coins, and she ran back to the phone. She dialed her home phone and got the answering machine. And then Mallorie remembered. Tonight was the night her parents played gin rummy with some other couples. They didn't usually get home until midnight.

I'll just walk home, Mallorie decided grimly. It was early enough that she could get home before her parents. She would already be showered and in bed by the time they got home. It was not really a bad walk except for the stretch of highway where there was no sidewalk. Most of the walk was through a nice residential area.

"Get your folks all right, little lady?" the bartender asked in a kindly voice.

"Yes, thank you," Mallorie said. She walked from the bar and headed home.

It won't be so hard, Mallorie told herself bravely. It will even be kind of pleasant. It's a bright, clear night and not too cold. The stars are out in abundance, and the moon is shining.

But then Mallorie got to the stretch of highway where cars and trucks were flying by too close for comfort. She had to walk in the deep brush and got thistles in her socks. She began to think of Vicky again.

Vicky, you dirtbag, Mallorie thought. You wanted to hurt me. You're an evil person. You didn't deserve the lead in the play. You don't deserve a guy like Brendon either. I hate you, Vicky Adams.

Mallorie was surprised by how easily she hated. It was such a good, almost energizing feeling. She had always felt sorry for people who let hatred into their hearts. Now she was one of them.

"No," Mallorie said aloud, "I don't hate you. You wanted to hurt me, but you failed. I don't hate you. It's kind of fun walking in the dark, hearing the crickets and the night birds. So you lost, Vicky. You didn't get me to hate you, and you didn't even ruin my night."

When Mallorie got to the residential area, she suddenly was struck by the sweetest smell she had ever experienced. The intensity of the perfume was almost overwhelming. "What is that?" she said aloud.

"Is that you, Mallorie McIntyre?" came

a familiar voice. It belonged to Abe Landers, the man who used to deliver mail in Mallorie's neighborhood. Abe and his wife Bertha often visited with Mallorie's family. Now Abe was out in his front yard watering the lawn.

"Yeah, it's me, Mr. Landers," Mallorie said.

"What're you doing walking around at this hour?" Mr. Landers asked as he aimed a spray of water at his shrubs. The evening was the best time to water on these warm September days.

"Oh, it's so nice out. I just thought I'd take a walk," Mallorie lied.

"Well, you be careful. It's a dangerous world out there," Mr. Landers said.

"What's that sweet smell?" Mallorie asked.

"Oh, that? Come here," he said. "It's my night-blooming cereus. See that big white flower there? It blooms at night and gives off that perfume. By morning it will be closed, and the blossom will never open again. All that beauty for one night's glory, eh?"

It wasn't too late yet, and Mallorie was

almost home, so she told Mr. Landers about the play she was in. "I have the female lead. It's really good. You and your wife should come see it."

"Well, we just might," Mr. Landers said. "You're at the Sierra Theater, eh? Well, good luck to you. A lot of misfortune has struck that place."

A chill ran down Mallorie's spine. "Misfortune? What kind of misfortune?" she asked.

"Oh, just a series of strange accidents, I guess. But such things often give rise to funny ideas, like that there's a curse or something. Not that I believe such things. I remember they were having this play, *The Ghost Sonata*, and a hanging took place in it. And darned if this pretty young girl who was playing in the thing didn't get tangled in the curtain ropes and hang herself. They found her hanging there, cold and dead in the morning," Mr. Landers said.

"How terrible," Mallorie said.

"Yeah. She was playing a character called The Lady in Black. Folks were wanting to close the theater after the hanging, but this eager playwright, Mr. Axton, was so determined that they kept it going. Did Shakespeare. Well, wouldn't you know the curse struck again," Mr. Landers said.

Mallorie stood listening, mesmerized. No wonder Mr. Axton had gotten so upset when she mentioned Vicky's story. A rumor like that could close the theater again, ruining everything he'd worked so hard for.

"*Macbeth* was the play. A pretty ambitious undertaking, *Macbeth*, using young kids for the acting. College kids— they were good. There was this little gal from the neighborhood, Cassie, Cassie Untermann. We all knew her—sweetest little thing. She had the part of Lady Macbeth, and darned if it didn't happen again—the curse or whatever. Cassie fell from the balcony in the Sierra Theater one night. Broke her neck. What a shocker that was. We all knew Cassie. We used to buy Girl Scout cookies from her . . ." Mr. Landers shook his head sadly. "She was growing up to be a beautiful young lady too. Only lived to be 19."

Mallorie stared at the old man. She recalled Vicky's story.

This crazed, lovesick young man hurled the object of his affection from the balcony, and she died of a broken neck . . . Then, according to Vicky, the killer escaped into the darkness, never to be seen again.

"Mr. Landers, were they sure those were accidents?" Mallorie asked in a shaky voice.

"Why, I expect so. The police must have investigated pretty well. Who knows, though," Mr. Landers said.

"And now I'm performing in that theater," Mallorie said.

Mr. Landers smiled. "Well, all this happened years ago. After Cassie died, they quit producing plays there. Mostly the place has been boarded up. Some homeless people have lived in there from time to time until the police chased them out. I was real surprised when I heard it was opening up again for plays. Yeah, me and Bertha might just come down to the theater to see you. What's the name of your play?"

"*The Werewolf of Warwick*. It sounds scary, but it's a comedy," Mallorie said.

"Well, Mallorie, just don't get too close to the curtain cords and stay away from the edge of the balcony," Mr. Landers said with a chuckle. "And then you'll be fine." He didn't seem to take the accidents of 20 years ago too seriously as curses or anything. He seemed to see them as tragic random happenings that had nothing to do with now.

Of course that was true, Mallorie told herself. Leave it to Vicky to make up her own version of the story.

Mallorie made it home before her parents by half an hour. She made herself a peanut butter sandwich and ate it with a glass of milk. Then she showered, got into her pajamas, and sat on top of her bed to study the playbook. She wasn't really very sleepy. And she had an awful lot to learn about playing Lady Cordelia.

As Mallorie was going over the scenes, the stories Mr. Landers told her kept recurring in her mind. The hanging. The fall from the balcony. Both of the victims had been young actresses. But that was just a coincidence.

Mallorie didn't believe in curses. She

had read all about the curse that was supposed to be on King Tutankhamen's tomb in Egypt. Everybody who had anything to do with finding the tomb seemed struck by disaster. But all the bad events had logical explanations. One man had died from pneumonia. Others had been murdered or had died of natural causes.

And there was surely no curse on the Sierra Theater! It was tragic that the girls had died, but a curse had nothing to do with it.

Mallorie focused once again on the play. The more she read the playbook, the more excited she became. She would have so much fun playing Lady Cordelia. Singing the duet near the end would be especially fun.

"I am hairy, I must say," Brendon would sing. "I lament I am this way."

Mallorie would respond, "Love conquers all, my furry sweet. It was fate that we should meet!"

Then together, arm in arm, they would sing, "Even werewolves fall in love, dance and dream 'neath stars above. Forgive the claws and pointy ears, smile awhile and calm your fears. A werewolf loved by one so fair has indeed a life to share!"

Mallorie smiled as she read the lyrics. They were corny, but it was still a wonderful play. It wasn't just about werewolves. It was about understanding people who are very different from the norm.

Mallorie was getting tired, so she put the playbook on her dressing table and started to climb into bed. Then she noticed that her curtains weren't completely closed, so she walked over to the window to close them.

She let out a short, startled cry.

A dark figure was sprinting over the lawn. Could it have been the man in black who had asked for change for coffee?

Had he been looking in her window?

5 MALLORIE WAS SHAKING as she checked all the windows and doors. They were all locked.

Had that strange man followed her home?

When Mallorie's parents came home, Mallorie rushed to meet them in the living room. "Mom! Dad! I think somebody was looking in my window. When I looked, he ran away across the lawn!"

"What?" Mr. McIntyre gasped.

Mallorie's mom rushed over and gave her a hug. "Honey, you should have called the police immediately if there was a prowler out there!"

"I was just so scared," Mallorie said. "I mean, I didn't expect to see anybody when I went to close the curtain, and I was just so shocked."

"Did you see a face looking in the window?" her dad asked.

"Well, no. But when I looked out the window, he seemed to be running from my window as if he'd been looking in,"

Mallorie said, realizing she was sounding very confused. Now Mallorie began to doubt herself. Her mind was so filled with stories of curses on the Sierra Theater, that strange beggar in town, the werewolf theme of the play, and Vicky's bitterness. Maybe she was imagining things. Maybe that person had not been at the window at all. Maybe it had just been a jogger taking a shortcut across the McIntyre lawn.

"Honey," her father said softly, "if there was a prowler here, then we need to call the police. Tell me exactly what you are sure of."

"Well," Mallorie said shakily, "I went to the window to close the drapes, and I saw this dark figure sprinting over our lawn toward the sidewalk. Oh, Dad, maybe it was nothing. The more I think about it, the sillier it seems. It's just that I've been rehearsing this weird play and hearing all kinds of wild rumors about the mysterious past of the Sierra Theater. Maybe my imagination is getting the best of me."

"I wish you weren't playing in such a sick production," Mrs. McIntyre said crossly. "I think it's beginning to put ideas into your head."

Even though Mallorie knew her mom was right about the play causing her imagination to go wild, she wasn't going to admit it. "It's not a sick play, Mom," Mallorie insisted. "It's a funny, cute play. And it has an important moral to it. It ends up saying that even very different people sometimes just need love and understanding."

"I'm sure!" her mother scoffed. "Hideous half-men, half-wolves who go around biting people need understanding. Well, I'll tell you this. They're not getting it from me!"

Mr. McIntyre smiled and winked at Mallorie behind her mom's back. "Heidi, sometimes you tell me I look like a werewolf when I don't shave, and I certainly need love and understanding!" he said.

Mrs. McIntyre made a face at him. "Don't joke about it. There are no such things as werewolves, anyway. Can't you be in a play that won't give you nightmares?" she said.

"Mom," Mallorie said, "werewolves are a metaphor for misunderstood people. Don't you see?"

"Oh, just do whatever you want, Mallorie. I'm too tired to argue about it," her mom said.

Mallorie's dad checked around the house, especially outside Mallorie's window, looking for signs of footprints or disturbed plants. Nothing was crushed or broken, and there were no prints in the soft soil. He was satisfied that no one had been peering in Mallorie's window, so he decided to just go to bed.

Mallorie was so upset by the night's events and her mom's distrust of the play that she had completely forgotten to tell her parents that she had gotten the lead role. Oh well, she thought. I'll just tell them later when all of this has blown over and Mom isn't so upset.

Mallorie slept fitfully that night. By dawn she was awake and determined not to let Vicky's spite or anything else spoil her joy at having the lead in the play. Playing Lady Cordelia was a dream come true, and Mallorie made up her mind to enjoy it to the fullest.

At school, Mallorie told her friend, Kelly, about what Vicky had done last night.

"I'm not surprised," Kelly said. "I never liked her. She can be really mean when she doesn't get her own way. When I was a freshman, some of us sat on the bleachers where her class sat, and she led the other girls in harassing us until we moved. I can imagine how spiteful she's going to be when you replace her in the lead of that play."

"Yeah," Mallorie said, "and it wasn't even my fault. The part fell into my lap when Vicky couldn't do it to Mr. Axton's liking."

"My sister was in Vicky's class," Kelly said. "At the graduation ceremony last year, Vicky almost ruined the whole thing. She made this big show of herself. She had organized this cheering section for herself in the bleachers, and they were blowing noisemakers and screaming and everything. They drowned out a lot of kids' names so nobody could hear them. Vicky was jumping around and acting so stupid that she turned the whole ceremony into a circus. She has always wanted to be the center of attention."

When Mallorie went to rehearsal that day, she cornered Cole immediately. She didn't want to risk another miserable walk down to the bus stop in the dark. "Hey, Cole, do you think it would be too much trouble if you dropped me off at my house after rehearsal tonight?" she asked.

Cole beamed. "Oh, no, not at all. I'd be glad to." Mallorie noticed then that he was kind of cute, even in his owlish glasses.

"Great," Mallorie said. "Thanks a lot."

"No problem," Cole said, still smiling. She hoped he wasn't reading anything into her request for a ride home. He was a nice guy and fun to work with on these plays and activities at school, but she just didn't see him as anything more than a friend. She hoped he would recognize that this was all it was—a friend asking another friend for a favor.

Brendon came up behind Mallorie without her noticing him. He wrapped his arms around her, giving her a squeeze. "Are you ready for our hot love scenes,

Lady Cordelia?" he asked, laughing.

Mallorie was startled by the bold gesture, but she liked it. She giggled and said, "I guess I'm ready."

"I'm really glad Axton gave you the female lead, Mallie," Brendon said. "You've got a lot more sparkle than Vicky has. You've got just what this role needs. Vicky was being too heavy, too humorless, too dramatic. This is not supposed to be a gloomy play."

Mallorie was surprised by Brendon's comments. Vicky was his girlfriend. They always came together when the rehearsals first started. It was a joke among the other cast members how they'd hide behind the curtains and make out during a lull in the rehearsals. Why would Brendon be so happy about a decision that brought his girlfriend so much pain and disappointment? That puzzled Mallorie.

"I was shocked when Mr. Axton gave the role to me," Mallorie said. "I mean, I thought it was all settled that Vicky would play Lady Cordelia."

Brendon grinned. "Axton asked me for my opinion before he made the decision.

He was having serious doubts about Vicky, but he said he wouldn't make the switch if I wasn't comfortable with it. I'm the star, you know. So Axton wasn't going to make the move without my approval," he said. Mallorie remembered Mr. Axton talking to Brendon before he went into the private office with Vicky.

"So . . . you said it would be okay to take Vicky out of the female lead?" Mallorie asked.

"Yeah. I could see the same problems Axton was seeing. She was in way over her head in a play like this," Brendon said.

Mallorie stared at Brendon, amazed at his indifferent attitude. "You know, Vicky is really upset. She's not even here yet, and she was always so early and anxious to get started. You know how sad she is, don't you?" Mallorie asked.

Brendon shrugged. "Life is tough. You have to learn to take disappointments," he said.

"Brendon, you two are . . . dating, aren't you? Vicky told me you two were really close, and it sure looked like it a couple weeks ago," Mallorie said.

"We hung out together, yeah. We went on a couple dates, but it's no big, serious relationship, Mallie. Maybe Vicky thought it was, but it never was for me. Man, I'm not going to be ready for anything serious for a long time. No way. I just want to have fun. But you know how Vicky can be. She blows things out of proportion," Brendon said.

Wow, Mallorie thought. Vicky's world is really falling apart. First, she loses the role she loved so much in the play, and now it looks like she didn't even have the boyfriend she thought she had.

Mallorie almost felt sorry for Vicky. Almost. Then she remembered the dirty trick Vicky had played on her. Being stranded at the lonely bus stop three miles from home was not fun, and the bitter, unfair things Vicky had said to her were hard to forget.

Maybe, Mallorie thought, Vicky deserved the run of bad luck she was having. Maybe somehow it would humble her and make her a better person.

Mallorie found an open dressing room and changed into her costume. Vicky finally showed up for the rehearsal, wearing a dark, drab dress in keeping with her new role of Hortense, the aging owner of the boardinghouse where John Winston lived. Vicky spotted Mallorie and said in a catty voice, "Did you finally get home last night? You know, I'm sorry I couldn't give you that ride I promised, but I remembered that I needed to pick up some of my friends, and I didn't have room in the car for a snake."

"Whatever," Mallorie snapped.

Hatred flashed in Vicky's eyes. "Look at you in that outrageous dress. You look ridiculous, do you know that?" Vicky laughed out loud. "Actually, you look hilarious. The play is supposed to take place in the middle 1700s, and you're wearing some stupid big dress that belonged to the Victorian era. Mr. Axton is going to be so disgusted that you didn't even bother to research the costumes of the period before you went to a Halloween store to buy that freaky dress."

Mallorie had dragged Kelly along to several costume stores, and together they had picked out this long, bouffant pale blue dress with a scoop neckline. It fit Mallorie's slim figure well, and she and Kelly thought she looked terrific. The clerk in the store had said the dress was ideal for 18th-century plays, and Mallorie had felt supremely confident. Until now. Now she felt terrible. Vicky had succeeded in undermining her confidence.

"You'll be the laughingstock of the whole town if you try to wear that dress," Vicky said.

Just then, Brendon came over. "Who's going to be a laughingstock?" he asked.

"Oh, Brendon." Vicky's tone of voice suddenly became sweet. "I was just trying to spare Mallorie a ton of embarrassment. Look at the dress she chose for Lady Cordelia. I mean, like a fashionable woman in the 18th century would be wearing that!"

Brendon turned to Mallorie and looked at the dress.

"I disagree," Brendon said. "I think Mallorie's dress is perfect. You look awesome, Mallorie, and that's just what Lady Cordelia would have been wearing in those days. But not many ladies in the

18th or any century would look as good as you do in the dress!"

Vicky looked as if Brendon had drawn a fish from a stinking barrel of rotting seafood and whipped her across the face with it. Mallorie had never seen such a hurt and shocked expression on anyone's face before. Vicky was totally caught off guard. Once again Mallorie was tempted to feel sorry for Vicky, but she refused the impulse. Vicky's unkindness made compassion impossible.

"Now, if you can act and sing as good as you look, Mallorie, we're on a roll," Brendon said, taking Mallorie's hand and squeezing it. Then he walked away to put on his costume.

Even though Mallorie loved the attention Brendon was giving her, she wondered if he knew what he was doing to Vicky. Didn't he care?

Vicky, her face distorted with rage, turned to Mallorie. Vicky was a beautiful girl, but her fury made her look like a psycho. "I told you what happened to one leading lady in this theater, didn't I?" she asked.

"Yes, but what you said wasn't true. She wasn't murdered by a lovesick guy like you said. It was an accident," Mallorie said.

"Really? And what about the other girl? I bet you don't know about the other girl."

"Yeah, I know about that too. There were two bad accidents 20 years ago, but it has nothing to do with now," Mallorie said.

"One of the leading ladies was hanged, and the other one died of a broken neck," Vicky said in a spiteful tone. "I wonder what will happen to you? You know, I'm glad I've got just a minor part in the play now. Bad things don't happen to the minor players, just to the stars! You know what, Mallorie? Maybe someday the ghost voice that calls for Cassandra will be calling your name. 'Mallorie . . . Mallorie . . .' Wouldn't that be a scream? I mean, wouldn't it just be hilarious?" Vicky's laughter was like a madwoman's shriek, sending cold chills down Mallorie's spine.

Mallorie turned her back on Vicky and walked over to Brendon. They were ready to rehearse one of their big scenes. Mallorie wanted to be really up for it. But Vicky's hatred poisoned the air, making Mallorie nauseous. Was Vicky threatening her?

6 DESPITE VICKY'S RAGE, Mallorie's scenes with Brendon went very well. Mr. Axton never detected the confusion in Mallorie's heart.

"Now everything is coming together," Mr. Axton cried. "We shall be ready for our opening, which will be here before we know it!"

As soon as Mallorie changed from her costume back into jeans and a T-shirt for the trip home, Cole was there. "Let's go," he said cheerfully.

"This is really nice of you, Cole. I hope it's not too far out of your way," Mallorie said.

"No, no. My pleasure," he said eagerly.

"I used to walk down to the bus stop, but sometimes it's freaky on the dark streets," Mallorie said. "There's one guy on the street in front of the discount store. He's dressed all in dark clothes and asks for change for coffee all the time. It kind of scares me because he looks so weird. His eyebrows seem to go all the way across his face . . . like . . . a werewolf!"

"Oh, that's Skipper," Cole said, walking beside Mallorie to his car.

"You know him?" Mallorie asked in surprise.

"Yeah. A long time ago some guys beat him with a crowbar. They broke his nose and left a scar across the top that makes his eyebrows look like that. He's one of the homeless guys who comes to my mom's bakery. He's always there early in the morning with the other ones, sniffing the good smells. Mom gives them day-old donuts and coffee. The bakery goods are still tasty, and the people appreciate getting something for free," Cole said.

"Oh, then he's harmless," Mallorie said. "The other day when I was walking home, he followed me, and I was so scared. I took a different route just to avoid him. And then I thought he was out in my neighborhood, but I was probably just imagining things."

Cole unlocked his car. "I can't see him getting way out to where you live, but he'll follow people begging for money. He'll do that. He's been arrested a lot of times when people complain, but then they just send him to mental health, and he's back on the street the next day. Guys like him, they just sort of fall through the cracks," Cole said, sadly shaking his head.

"How old is he?" Mallorie wondered.

"Probably 40-something. He looks younger because he's so skinny. Like me, I guess. Everybody thinks I'm a freshman at Kennedy, and here I am—a senior! Skipper has been hanging around here for as long as I can remember and probably before that too," Cole said.

Mallorie looked out on the deserted street as they drove. From the safety of Cole's car, everything looked different. "Look, there he is, Cole," she said, pointing to the odd man dressed all in black.

"Yeah," Cole said. "When the Sierra Theater was closed, he and his friends would spend the night in there. They'd crawl up to the balcony and sleep. It'd be pretty cozy. It was a good place for homeless people to hang out. Now they don't have anywhere to go."

"Cole," Mallorie said, remembering the story Mr. Landers had told. "Did you ever hear about the curse of the Sierra Theater? The old legends about those two deaths?"

"Sure. Everybody who's lived in town very long knows that story. It all happened when our parents were our ages now, so it was a big thing," Cole said.

"That was awful how those two girls got killed, huh?" Mallorie said.

"Yeah. One of them was my mom's best friend. Cassie Untermann and my mom were really close. They graduated together from Kennedy High. They were the first graduating class from our high school. Mom told me it hit her really hard when Cassie died," Cole said.

"Everybody is sure it was an accident, right?" Mallorie asked.

Cole suddenly gripped the steering wheel more tightly and took a quick look at Mallorie. "Of course. What else would it be?"

"Oh, you know, I heard some weird story about some rejected lover pushing the girl over the edge of the balcony," Mallorie said. "But that's silly, huh?"

"I never heard that," Cole said, "but it

sounds pretty far-fetched." He looked at Mallorie again. "You sure sounded great in rehearsal tonight. Mr. Axton was just all smiles. You have a really beautiful voice. And you looked good too."

"Oh, thanks, Cole," Mallorie said. She wished he wouldn't say nice things to her like that. She liked the compliments but didn't want Cole obsessing over her.

"I'm sure glad we're working together on the play," Cole said. "The last project we did together was that Thanksgiving basket thing right after you moved here. We chaired that, remember? It was the biggest food drive Kennedy High had ever had. We got more baskets to the needy than anyone else ever had."

"Yeah, that was fun," Mallorie admitted. She and Cole had done a lot of laughing as they sorted tons of cans of pumpkin pie mix, cranberries, and yams so every family got enough of everything. Brendon would probably never volunteer his free time for charity like that.

When Mallorie got home, her dad was in the living room. "How did the rehearsal go?" he asked.

"Oh, it was great. I have the lead now with Brendon Hayes, so it's really fun," Mallorie said.

"Oh? What happened to the other girl?" he asked. "Did she get sick or something?"

"No. Mr. Axton decided she couldn't handle it," Mallorie said.

"Oh, by the way, honey, you got a package today. It's on the kitchen table. It looks like flowers. Maybe your playwright, that Mr. Axton, is sending you flowers to congratulate you on getting the lead in the play," Mallorie's father said, smiling.

Mallorie walked into the kitchen and stared a moment at the box. Something did not seem right. Mr. Axton wouldn't be sending flowers now. If the play was a big success, he would, but not now. And the ribbon that tied the box shut was kind of crumpled and dirty.

Mallorie picked up the box and carried it to her bedroom. She wanted to be alone when she opened it in case it was something upsetting. Her mom was against the play anyway, and Mallorie didn't want anything else to tick her off.

Mallorie cut the ribbon and opened the

box slowly. She gasped when she saw the contents.

Mr. McIntyre had noiselessly come up behind Mallorie and was now looking over her shoulder. "What the heck is that?" he cried.

A dozen roses, very dead, curled, and black, lay in the box tied with a rope that resembled a noose.

"It's a sick joke," Mallorie said weakly.

"I'll say," her father agreed. "Mallorie, let me take the box out to the trash. There are bugs crawling in there."

Mallorie took the card out and let her father grab the box and hurry out to the trash. Mallorie stood there, sick at the thought of Vicky taking the trouble to find 12 dead roses and then to catch bugs and put them in the box to make it more disgusting. And the noose . . .

It had to be Vicky who did this. It had to be.

Mallorie read the typed card.

The Lady in Black never came back,
Hanged by the neck, she was a wreck.
Cassandra fell from way up high,

Cassandra was too young to die.
All good things come in threes they say,
Will Mallorie be the one to die today?

And along with the poem, there was a business card from a local mortuary.

Flooded with anger, Mallorie called Vicky's house. Vicky's mother answered.

"I need to talk to Vicky right away, Mrs. Adams," Mallorie said.

When Vicky came on the line, she said "Hi" in a breezy voice.

"Vicky, I got your disgusting dead roses and the stupid poem. I just want to tell you something, Vicky, and you'd better listen. I'm sick of you harassing me. This is just too much. I won't stand for it anymore. The next dirty thing you do to me, I'm telling Mr. Axton and Brendon and everybody else, maybe even the police!" With that, Mallorie banged down the receiver.

Mallorie threw the poem away and went to study for an upcoming math test. She wanted to forget everything about the play for a while. She'd been doing problems for ten minutes when the phone rang.

"Mallorie, this is Brendon," the voice on the line said. "Since we don't have rehearsals tomorrow night, what do you say we go somewhere for fun?"

Mallorie was kind of surprised. Each day things had grown more and more flirtatious between them, but she just thought it was all in fun. Mallorie had always been blown away by Brendon. From the first moment she met him, she thought that dating him would be incredible. Now her heart raced with excitement. "Yeah, sure, Brendon. That would be great," she said.

"Okay! I'll pick you up around 7:00 tomorrow," Brendon said. "We'll decide where to go from there. Just a go-with-the-flow type of deal, okay?"

"Yeah, that's cool," Mallorie said. She was shaking all over. It wasn't as if this was her first date. But Brendon was in college. He was so handsome, so sophisticated. He had already done a few bit parts in television soap operas. A few weeks ago, Mallorie would have considered herself lucky to have him just smile at her!

Now Brendon was asking her out on a date!

"Just think," Brendon said before he hung up, "you're having a date with a werewolf, Mallorie."

"But a nice werewolf," Mallorie managed to quip.

"Just wait until you hear me howl," he laughed.

After he hung up, Mallorie leaped onto her bed, hugged her knees to her chest, and squealed with joy. "Oh," she said to herself, "this is so awesome!"

Vicky, of course, would be more enraged than ever. But that didn't worry Mallorie anymore. Vicky was a mean-spirited, spiteful girl, and maybe when she realized it was totally over between her and Brendon, she'd drop out of the play entirely, and Mallorie would be rid of her. Mallorie didn't plan to attend the local college Vicky went to, so with a little bit of luck, their paths would never cross again.

Oh wow, oh wow, Mallorie thought.

Just then she saw a large black bug slowly making its way across her pearl-colored carpet—a big, disgusting cockroach!

It must have escaped from the box before her dad took it outside.

It was as if Vicky had managed to ruin even this moment of triumph with something ugly and frightening.

7 BRENDON ARRIVED at Mallorie's house the following evening and wowed her parents by coming in and making intelligent small talk with them before he left with Mallorie. She could tell he had made a great impression.

Once in the car, Brendon said, "So, Lady Cordelia, where shall we go?"

"You pick something, and I'll love it," Mallorie said.

"The girl is a dream," Brendon laughed. "Okay, we'll pick up a chicken basket at the Hennery, and then we'll go listen to a band from my college perform on the green, under the stars. How does that sound?"

"Fabulous," Mallorie said.

They bought a basket of fried chicken, mashed potatoes, cole slaw, and apple pie, and then they found a comfortable spot on the hill to listen to a loud rock group composed of Brendon's friends. It was the most wonderful date Mallorie had ever had.

On the way home, Brendon said, "Lady Cordelia, I could get used to you."

"I like you too, John Winston," Mallorie said, going along with the joke.

"You see? The lyrics are true, even if they are a little corny. Werewolves do fall in love," Brendon said.

On the way to Mallorie's house, they passed the Sierra Theater and noticed some excitement around the building. The police were there, along with a small crowd.

"Brendon! Look! I wonder what's going on," Mallorie said.

Brendon pulled to the curb halfway down the block. "Let's go see," he said.

Mr. Axton was standing outside the theater, looking very agitated.

"What's going on, Mr. Axton?" Brendon asked.

"Someone broke into the theater tonight," Mr. Axton said. "The police are in there now getting him out. Somebody heard breaking glass and called the police. Oh, this is dreadful. I hope he didn't harm anything. Everything was going so well for our opening night!"

The police came out then, leading a

handcuffed man between them.

"It's that guy who kept asking me for money for coffee when I walked to the bus stop after rehearsals," Mallorie said. "Cole knows him. He said his name is Skipper."

Brendon scowled. "One of those homeless losers! There are too many of his kind on the streets. They should be locked up somewhere. That guy has been a plague on the neighborhood for years," he said.

"Cole said he's harmless," Mallorie said.

"Well, he's not," Brendon snapped, showing more temper than Mallorie had seen before. "None of them are. You never know what they'll do next. Why do we have to put up with them?"

Mr. Axton checked the inside of the theater and found nothing stolen or damaged. But they put Skipper in the police car anyway for breaking a back window and crawling into the theater.

"It's my home," Skipper was mumbling. "I been there a long time. You can ask anybody. I don't know why they locked me out of my own home."

"It's not your home," Mr. Axton said

crossly. "Just because you and some other bums lived there when the theater was closed is no reason to trespass now."

"I pay rent every month," Skipper insisted. "I got a disability check. I pay rent."

One of the police officers grimaced and said, "I don't think so, buddy."

A terrible thought came to Mallorie's mind, but she didn't say it. Had Skipper been staying in the theater 20 years ago? Had he snuck in when those other plays were being staged? Could he have come into his "home" late at night and mistook a young actress for an intruder and pushed her over the balcony?

....

The next day after school, Mallorie accessed old newspapers to read about the deaths of Cassandra Untermann and Jayne Lawson. She had gotten those names from Mr. Landers and from looking in the yearbooks at Kennedy High.

"Actress Dies in Local Theater," the headline read. The story described the tragic circumstances of Jayne Lawson's death.

"Jayne was appearing in *The Ghost Sonata* at the Sierra Theater. Late last night she was alone in the theater where she had gone to rehearse when she became tangled in the curtain ropes. Her alarmed parents reported her missing when she failed to return home. A search led to the discovery of her hanged body."

Mallorie felt numb as she moved on to find the details of Cassandra Untermann's death.

"Local Girl Dies in Fall from Theater Balcony," the headline read. Mallorie read the article. "Recent Kennedy High School graduate Cassandra Untermann was rehearsing her role as Lady Macbeth in the Sierra Theater last night. Her parents reported her missing early this morning, and police found her body where she had fallen from the balcony. A broken railing in the balcony may have been the cause of the accident."

Mallorie found more articles describing the funerals of the girls and then later articles remarking about the eerie coincidences of the two deaths. Much-later articles commented on the boarded-up theater and various plans to reopen it as an auction house, warehouse, or store. One article, printed on Halloween, made reference to "the curse of the Sierra Theater."

None of the stories hinted at foul play.

But what if Skipper had surprised both girls and somehow caused their deaths? Mallorie didn't mention her fear to anyone. She didn't want to get an innocent man in trouble over a wild theory. In all likelihood, Skipper was just what Cole had said he was—a poor, harmless soul caught up in a world he would never function in or understand. There were a lot like him. A long time ago such people were locked up in hospitals. But things had changed, and now most every city had its share of bewildered men and women pushing shopping carts filled with their worldly possessions, sleeping on sidewalks, begging, mumbling, struggling.

Something should be done about these people, but Mallorie didn't know the right thing to do. It wasn't their fault, for the most part, that they were like that, so they needed compassion.

But what if Skipper was dangerous? What if Brendon was right . . .

....

When Mallorie arrived for rehearsals the next night, she told Cole about seeing Skipper being arrested.

"Yeah, I know. Poor guy. They won't keep him long though. He's not a criminal. He's always in and out of jail, and then they send him to mental health. They check that he's taking his medicine, which he usually isn't, and then he's out on the street again. Probably tomorrow morning he'll be lined up as usual with the others getting his donut and coffee at my mom's bakery," Cole said with a smile, as if he hoped that would be the case. Cole definitely had a lot of sympathy for Skipper.

"Cole, you sure he wouldn't . . . you know . . . hurt anybody? I mean, something is wrong with him. Is it possible he'd get confused and hurt somebody, even, like, by mistake?" Mallorie asked.

"Skipper?" Cole laughed. "He wouldn't hurt a fly. The guy is an innocent little kid at heart. He didn't even realize he was breaking into that theater. He thought somebody had locked his house, and all he knew was that he needed to go home."

Maybe, Mallorie thought darkly, Skipper didn't even realize he was hurting those girls when he choked one and pushed the other one off the balcony.

Rehearsal went well, and Mr. Axton was thoroughly impressed with how quickly Mallorie had learned the part of Lady Cordelia. To top the night off, Vicky didn't say one word to Mallorie, which was perfectly fine with her.

Cole drove Mallorie home again after rehearsals.

"You like jazz, don't you, Mallorie?" he asked.

"Uh, yeah," Mallorie said, sensing what was coming.

"There's a really cool jazz festival downtown on Sunday," Cole said.

"Oh, yeah? I wish I could go, but the family is getting together for a barbecue and stuff, and I'll be real busy," Mallorie said.

"Oh," Cole said. "Well, they'll have a

few more jazz weekends. Maybe later on you'll have some free time, and we can go. I know you'd have a lot of fun. They've got a lot of street vendors selling great food, and the whole atmosphere is just amazing."

Mallorie thanked Cole for the ride and hurried inside. She felt like a jerk. She knew she should just be straightforward with him, telling him she just wanted to be friends, but she just couldn't bring herself to do it.

When Mallorie got inside, her mother greeted her with a serious look on her face. She didn't ask how the rehearsal went or anything. "Mallorie, I need to talk to you," she said.

"Okay, Mom," Mallorie said, following her mother to the sofa.

"Right after I got home from work, I got this very disturbing call from Irene Adams, Vicky's mother. She's really worried about her daughter. She said Vicky has always been such an optimistic, upbeat girl, but now she has sunk into this deep depression, and her mother said it has to do with things you are doing to her," Mrs.

McIntyre said. "It came as a complete shock to me because I didn't even know you and Vicky had anything to do with each other. You never talk about her."

"Well, it's not my fault if she's depressed," Mallorie said defensively. "I had this little bitty part in the play, and I was perfectly happy with it, and Vicky had the lead. Then Mr. Axton didn't like the way Vicky was acting, so he asked me to take the lead. That's all. I never tried to take it away from her. It just happened."

"Mallorie, you never told me you replaced another girl in the play. You never said anything about it," her mom said in an accusing tone.

"Dad knows. I told him," Mallorie said. "You just didn't seem interested in the play and what was going on, Mom. It's no big deal anyway."

Mrs. McIntyre's eyebrows shot up. "Yes, it is a big deal! Irene Adams said that role meant the world to her daughter. She even sewed these elaborate costumes for the part. Irene said Vicky had never been so excited in her whole life about anything as she was about being the lead in that play."

"Mom! What did she expect me to do?" Mallorie cried. "Mr. Axton didn't want her to play Lady Cordelia anymore because she was no good. It wasn't my fault!"

"But, poor Vicky," Mrs. McIntyre lamented. "It just sent her into a downward spiral . . ."

"Don't feel sorry for her, Mom. She's mean and hateful. She's been harassing me ever since it happened. You know that big box that came the other day? You thought it was flowers. Well, it was a bunch of rotting dead roses filled with bugs from Vicky, and she even put in a horrible poem and a business card from a mortuary!" Mallorie said.

Her mom looked alarmed. "Mallorie! This is terrible!" she cried. "You are involved in such an awful situation. It's the fault of that twisted play! You're doing a sick play about a werewolf, and all kinds of horrible things are happening. I just wish you'd drop the whole thing!"

"Mom! I love being in the play, and it's not twisted. Vicky is the only horrible thing! I'm thrilled to be playing the lead. I didn't go out for it, but now that I have it, I love it. Mom, you know I've always dreamed of being an actor. I've had this dream since I was eight years old. This could be the beginning of something wonderful for me—the chance of a lifetime. If the play gets good reviews and stuff, and if they like my work, I could come to the attention of important people in the theater world. Do you think I'm going to let that hateful little brat spoil my chances?" Mallorie cried.

Her mom's eyes narrowed. "Mallorie, that doesn't sound like you. You've always been such a sweet girl who makes friends with everyone you meet. Now you're starting to sound like Vicky—so determined to be the best that you don't care who you hurt along the way."

8

"THIS IS SO UNFAIR," Mallorie wailed, "so totally unfair!"

"What's all the yelling about?" Mr. McIntyre asked, coming into the room.

"Dad! Mom's mad at me for taking the lead in the play when Mr. Axton asked me to take it. He didn't want Vicky Adams, and if I had turned him down, he would have just gotten another girl. Why was it so wrong for me to take the opportunity?" Mallorie asked.

Mallorie's mom looked at her husband and said, "Vicky's mother called. The girl is almost on the verge of a nervous breakdown. That lead meant so much to her. I just feel bad that Mallorie is in the middle of such a bad situation."

"Yeah, but like Mallorie said, she didn't look for the role. It just fell into her lap," Mallorie's father said. "She had every right to take it. Vicky is being a spoiled brat."

Mallorie looked gratefully at her father. "And that's not all, Dad. She's done so many hateful things to me since I got the lead. Remember that box of roses, Dad. You saw it. Well, that was from Vicky!" Mallorie said.

"That was sick," he said, shaking his head. He put his arms around Mrs. McIntyre's shoulders and said softly, "Let's just let Vicky's mom deal with Vicky's tantrums. It will all blow over."

Mallorie went to her room. The emotional outburst had worn her out. She flopped down on her bed and stared at the ceiling.

Mallorie kept saying to herself, It's not my fault . . . It's not my fault. . . .

But then a sick feeling of guilt swept over Mallorie. Her fault or not, she was demolishing Vicky Adams' life. She took her role in the play, and now she was taking her boyfriend. Only a few weeks ago, Vicky had been on top of the world. She had been Lady Cordelia in *The Werewolf of Warwick* and had been in Brendon's arms.

Now Mallorie had everything.

Mallorie reached for her phone and called Kelly. She always gave Mallorie her honest opinion when Mallorie asked her for advice.

"Kelly, I had to take the part, didn't I? It wasn't my fault Mr. Axton picked me," Mallorie groaned to her friend.

"You're right," Kelly said. "Just blow it off."

"Kelly," Mallorie said then, "there's something else . . . I mean, I haven't told you about this. You know Brendon, that really gorgeous guy who plays the werewolf? Well, I've always been crazy about him, but I never did anything because he was Vicky's boyfriend, and I wouldn't steal another girl's guy. But, Kelly, Brendon told me he really isn't serious about Vicky, and he asked me out."

"You didn't go out with him, did you?" Kelly asked.

"Well, uh . . . he said there was nothing between him and Vicky," Mallorie said evasively.

"Mallie! You did go out with him, didn't you? Now you shouldn't have done that," Kelly scolded.

"But Kelly, Brendon said—" Mallorie argued.

"Never mind what that guy said. You

knew he was Vicky's boyfriend, and you just don't move in like that. You should have at least waited until the play was over. Can you imagine what it's like for Vicky to see you two together? You playing her role and cuddling with her boyfriend? That's harsh, Mallie. That's something she would do, not you," Kelly said.

Mallorie was shaken. She was being insensitive. She realized that now. She decided she wouldn't go out with Brendon again until the play was over. She would keep their relationship at the theater professional. If Brendon wanted to date Mallorie when Vicky was completely out of the picture, that would be different.

....

The next day, Kelly drove Mallorie over to the college where Brendon attended drama classes. Rehearsals didn't start until 7:00, so they had plenty of time.

When Brendon saw Mallorie, he came over, smiling. "Hey, Lady Cordelia, what a nice surprise!"

They sat under the shade of a jacaranda tree and talked. "Brendon, Vicky has been really mad about losing the lead in the play, and she doesn't really like us dating either. Her mom called my mom and said she's having a nervous breakdown or something," Mallorie said.

"No kidding?" Brendon said. "How juvenile."

"Brendon, I was just thinking, maybe we should keep our relationship professional until the play ends. When Vicky sees us flirting, I guess it tears her up," Mallorie said.

Brendon looked angry. He had a low boiling point. "Well, she can just have her nervous breakdown for all I care. I don't intend to change my life for some high-strung spoiled brat. That's what turned me off about her in the first place. She was acting like she owned me. Forget her. I've got news for the psycho chick. I don't belong to her, and I never did. I like you, Mallorie, and I don't intend to hide that fact from anybody," he said.

"Brendon, I just don't want any trouble," Mallorie said.

"Trust me. When I'm done talking to her, she won't bother either of us anymore. I'll set Vicky Adams straight," Brendon said, grasping Mallorie's hands and smiling warmly. "We got something good going, babe, and nobody is going to take that away from us. On my way to rehearsals tonight, I'll stop at Vicky's house and tell her what's up."

"Brendon, she's going to—" Mallorie began.

Brendon reached out with his fingers and touched Mallorie's lips. "Shhhh, not to worry," he said softly.

And then he kissed Mallorie. It was not the quick kisses he had put on her cheek before. It was a warm, fierce kiss on the lips that sent Mallorie reeling.

As Mallorie headed back to Kelly's car, she was fearful. But slowly, anger replaced the fear. Why should she be intimidated by Vicky Adams? As Kelly drove to the theater, Mallorie told her, "Brendon is right. Why should Vicky ruin it for us? I'm glad he's going to talk to her. That's the best way. Just cut it off. Then maybe she'll quit the play, and we'll both be rid of her."

"Girl, you're cold," Kelly said.

Mallorie turned her head sharply. "Kelly,

that's not fair. I haven't done anything wrong!"

"Mallie, just turn the tables for a minute and imagine how you'd feel. A cute little girl comes and steals your role in the play and takes your boyfriend away from you all in a few days' time!" Kelly said.

"I wouldn't want a part in a play if I couldn't do it well, and I wouldn't want a boyfriend who didn't want me," Mallorie cried.

Kelly dropped Mallorie off at the theater. In spite of Mallorie's brave, strident talk, she was scared. She hurried toward the door of the Sierra Theater, not looking right or left. Suddenly a slurred voice called out, "Got change for coffee?"

Cole was right. Skipper was back, right here in front of the theater now. Mallorie fumbled in her purse. She found three quarters. As she started to put them into the man's grimy hand, two of them dropped. Both Mallorie and the man stooped to get them, and their heads touched. Skipper had long, dirty brown hair with long tendrils that streamed down his back. He was dirty and weird, and

Mallorie wanted no contact with him.

"Just don't touch me!" Mallorie hissed, recoiling from the man's touch, from his smell.

"S—sorry," Skipper mumbled.

"Just take the money and go," Mallorie cried.

"You're mean," he said in his slurred speech. "Girls are mean . . ." His eyes seemed to glow with animosity. He rocked back and forth on his heels and kept muttering, "Mean, mean . . ."

Mallorie backed away in horror. She thought about Jayne and Cassandra 20 years ago. Had Skipper looked at them like he was looking at Mallorie? Had they recoiled in fear and disgust, angering him? And since he was alone in the theater, did he hurt them for being "mean"?

Mallorie ran into the theater without looking back.

9 MR. AXTON WAS ON the phone when Mallorie came in. He was having an angry conversation. "I cannot believe this. This is so unprofessional. No, it is not a small, insignificant part. Hortense has some important narration that ties the acts together. I cannot believe this, Vicky. I thought you were a professional!"

Mallorie stood listening in silence.

Vicky was quitting! It was what she had hoped for. Brendon must have talked to her right after leaving class, and that had been the last straw. He was probably very blunt. Vicky couldn't bear the pain anymore of seeing him and Mallorie as a couple.

Mallorie wasn't sure how she felt. There was relief.

And there was guilt.

When Brendon arrived, he walked over to Mallorie. "She's gone, you know," he said with satisfaction.

"Was it awful talking to her, Brendon?"

Mallorie asked. "I mean, did she cry and stuff, or did she seem okay with you know . . . everything?" Mallorie wanted some crumb of comfort about all this, something to relieve her guilt.

"Not to worry," Brendon said. "She's history. Let's rehearse."

The rehearsal went beautifully in spite of the queasy feeling in Mallorie's stomach. They ended with Brendon's and Mallorie's cheesy love song duet.

"Dear Cordelia, you set this heart aflame. I am set to yearning at the mention of your name!"

Mallorie responded in her pure soprano, "Likewise Johnny dear, you are quite the dashing lad. My poor heart is reeling. I am going mad!"

Brendon put his arms around Mallorie, and she was swept into the magic of the deep brown eyes she had fallen for during that first day as Brendon sang, "You are mine forever, no matter what they say. Love has conquered fear, so let us sail away!"

Mr. Axton and the other cast members applauded.

Brendon and most of the others left then, leaving just Mr. Axton, Cole, and Mallorie in the theater. Cole hung around to make sure Mallorie had her ride home.

The phone rang then, and Cole answered it. He looked very serious as he spoke. "Yes, of course. I understand. I'm sure it will be okay." He put down the phone and said, "I'll lock up tonight, Mr. Axton. That was Vicky Adams on the phone. She's, uh . . . embarrassed to come by when everybody's here, but she wants to pick up her two dresses, the ones she, you know, made when she was Lady Cordelia."

Mr. Axton frowned then nodded. "I'm sure she doesn't want to face me after quitting like that. Well, no matter. Perhaps it's best she quit after being so bitter about losing the lead. I'm sorry for her disappointment, but the play is most important. Give her the dresses and tell her no hard feelings," he said.

Mr. Axton left, and Cole went to the costume closet for Vicky's dresses. "She sure went to a lot of trouble making these," Cole said, taking them down gently. Purple satin with black velvet trim. "It's gorgeous. Man, she must have worked for hours and hours on these." There was a thread of sorrow in Cole's voice.

Even Mallorie felt sad. She imagined Vicky slaving over her sewing machine, hour after hour, lovingly making the dresses for her glorious performance as the female star of the play. "It's too bad it all happened like it did," Mallorie said.

"Vicky feels awful about losing the part, doesn't she?" Cole asked.

"How do you know?" Mallorie asked. As far as she knew, Vicky never talked much to Cole.

"Her mom and my mom are friends," Cole said. "Vicky's mom always comes in the bakery to get apple strudel. She said Vicky is crushed. The play was all she talked about before. She had a big scrapbook all ready for the publicity pictures, the reviews." Cole briefly closed his eyes, took off his glasses, and rubbed a red spot on the bridge of his nose. When he turned toward Mallorie, he looked rather handsome.

"Cole," Mallorie said in a small, fearful

voice. "Do you think I did something bad in taking the part that belonged to Vicky? Am I a bad, selfish person?" Mallorie wanted so desperately to be reassured by someone she respected. And she did respect Cole.

"No, Mr. Axton just did not want her as Lady Cordelia," Cole said. "She would have lost out even if you had refused the part. I think what really tore her was, you know . . . the other stuff."

"What other stuff?" Mallorie asked shakily.

Cole shrugged. "You and Brendon. When we first started rehearsing the play, Vicky and Brendon would be hiding behind the curtains cuddling, whispering, looking into each other's eyes. Well, if she had had Brendon to fall back on, losing the role might not have thrown her so much, but it seemed like the minute she got dropped from the role, Brendon dropped her too," he said.

Mallorie felt worse than ever.

"Cole, I never wanted to hurt Vicky!"

Cole nodded. "I don't blame you. I blame him though. Brendon really didn't show a lot of class. You don't dump a girl who's reeling from a big disappointment and just flaunt your affection for another girl in her face. That was pretty bad," he said.

Tears began to run down Mallorie's face. "Oh, Cole, I shouldn't have been part of it. I should have realized that Vicky was hurting so badly and Brendon was off limits. I don't know what got into me. I just had this stupid crush on him, and when I got my chance, I just went for it!" she cried.

"You weren't thinking," Cole said kindly. "Sometimes people have that kind of effect on you." He lifted Vicky's dresses off the hangers and folded them into a large box, wrapping them in acid-free paper. He thought she'd want to just grab the box and go.

"Cole, what should I do to make it right?" Mallorie asked.

"Well, when Vicky shows up to get her dresses, just say you're sorry and you hope she's okay," Cole said.

"But what if she screams and yells at me?" Mallorie said.

"Would you feel better if I gave her the box and you stayed in the office and didn't see her?" Cole asked.

"Yeah, sure, but then afterward I'd feel even worse. I'd even be chickening out of the decency of an apology," Mallorie said. "No, I'll do it. In fact, Cole, why don't you go down to the snack shop and get some coffee? Give me maybe 30 minutes. I think it's better if it's just Vicky and me."

"You sure?" Cole asked.

"Yeah," Mallorie said.

Vicky arrived in about ten minutes. She was a tall girl, several inches taller than Mallorie, and heavier too. But she was very beautiful. Now she was wearing a red pullover and jeans, but her face was a portrait of sorrow. She wore no makeup. She looked as if she'd been crying nonstop for hours.

"Vicky, here's the box with your dresses in it," Mallorie said. "Cole fixed it for you. Vicky, I know you hate me, but I just want you to know I am so sorry for hurting you."

Vicky stood there in the semi-dark

theater, staring at Mallorie.

"I swear I never meant to hurt you," Mallorie said. "I wish now Mr. Axton had never picked me for Lady Cordelia. I wish nothing that has happened would have happened."

"It doesn't matter anymore," Vicky finally said.

"Vicky, Brendon isn't my boyfriend. I know that's what you think, and I did have a crush on him, but I could never like a guy like him. He's too selfish. I see him now for what he really is," Mallorie said.

"He came to see me today," Vicky said in a strange, flat voice. "He came to my house and said we needed to talk privately, so we went off in his car. You know, for a few insane moments, I thought he'd come back to me. But when he got me alone, he told me he didn't love me at all and I should just get out of his life. He told me I should quit the play because I was making you and him nervous. He told me that for all he cared, I could drop dead."

Vicky smiled then, like how a skull might smile. "Wasn't that sweet?" she asked.

"Vicky, I must have been crazy to ever like him," Mallorie said.

"Well, I've been hurt and humiliated so much that it doesn't really matter anymore. Where's Cole?" Vicky asked.

"I sent him down for coffee so we'd have time alone to talk," Mallorie said. "I wanted to tell you how truly awful I feel."

"You know, Mallorie, you are a good actress," Vicky said. "You are so convincing right now. If I didn't know better, I'd think you were really sorry for ruining my life, but I know better. You've enjoyed every minute of it. And tonight you and Brendon will be together laughing up a storm over all of this." There was a frightening glow to Vicky's eyes.

"You're w—wrong," Mallorie said. She became nervous then. Cole wasn't due back for 20 minutes. She had to get out of there. Now.

Mallorie started for the door, but Vicky lunged at her, throwing her down. She began to drag Mallorie up the stairs to the balcony.

When they got to the top of the stairs, Vicky hurled Mallorie into a dark corner with such force that it winded Mallorie.

"Vicky, noooo!" Mallorie screamed as the girl advanced toward her.

10

VICKY WRESTLED Mallorie to the floor, pulling her arms behind her back. She tied Mallorie's wrists together with rope from the green drapes.

Terrible thoughts crowded Mallorie's distracted mind. Jayne, the poor girl who was strangled by the ropes, probably died on this very spot! Vicky knew about that too. In her wild rage, maybe she was trying to make history repeat itself.

Mallorie remembered the lines from the poem Vicky put in the box of dead roses.

The Lady in Black never came back,
Hanged by the neck, she was a wreck . . .

"It must have been such fun watching me suffer as you and Brendon snuggled and smooched," Vicky snarled as she tightened the ropes on Mallorie's wrists so hard that pain shot up Mallorie's arms. "You saw it was eating me alive, and you didn't care."

"I'm sorry, I'm sorry, please believe me," Mallorie cried.

"Can you imagine how it felt to be playing that frump Hortense while you two were crooning love songs to each other? It was like a knife turning in my heart," Vicky said as she tied Mallorie's ankles together with more rope, again making the knots painfully tight.

Then Vicky deliberately tore a large piece of cloth from her own beautiful Lady Cordelia costume and violently stuffed it into Mallorie's mouth. Finally, using a satin strip, she secured the gag over Mallorie's face.

Mallorie pinned her hopes on Cole. He would be back soon. When he found Mallorie gone, he would get suspicious and come looking for her.

Vicky turned on the CD player, and music filled the theater. Then she cocked her head and said, "Uh-oh, there's Cole." She hurried down the stairs from the balcony to meet him.

"Hi, Vicky. Mallorie ready to go?" Cole asked.

"You're too late," Vicky said. "Brendon came and picked her up. Her new love. I guess they've got a big date."

"Oh," Cole said in a disappointed voice.

Mallorie tried desperately to make a noise, but all she could manage was a grunt, easily drowned out by the music Vicky had turned on. She tried to kick at something with her bound ankles, but she couldn't reach anything. Silently she begged, "Don't go, Cole, don't go without me . . . you must see she's lying . . ."

But then a door slammed, and Cole was gone.

Vicky came back up the stairs to the balcony. She was laughing. "He's gone, gone, gone, gone."

Vicky knelt down and grasped a handful of Mallorie's hair, giving it a painful shake. "What shall we do with you, Lady Cordelia? The curse of the Sierra Theater is about to strike for the third time, but how shall it be? Oh, this is so fun. Axton will lose his precious theater. It will close again like it did before when the accidents happened. They were accidents, but this will be no accident. Brendon will lose his new sweetie and the role of John Winston, which is so dear to him. And you . . . oh, yeah, I've saved the best for you."

Mallorie's eyes opened wide in terror as the girl came closer. "Shall I push you off the balcony like Cassandra? Or shall I rig a little noose so you swing like The Lady in Black did? Or shall I shove you in the costume closet and start a lovely fire?"

Just then, Mallorie heard the sound of glass breaking. A tiny ray of hope came into her heart—any distraction was welcome as Vicky plotted her death.

Vicky stood up, annoyance on her face. "What's that?" she muttered. She went down the stairs into the theater, and Mallorie heard her say, "What are you doing in here, you dirty bum? The cops got you once for breaking in here. You get out of here now, you hear me?"

Mallorie tried frantically again to swing her bound feet into some object to make a noise.

"This is my house," Skipper mumbled in his slurred voice. "I pay rent. I get a disability check, and I pay rent."

"You're crazy!" Vicky shrieked. "Get out of here!"

Mallorie struggled until she felt a chair at her feet. She tried with all her strength to kick it. It toppled over, making a loud noise.

"Who's up there in my balcony?" Skipper demanded. "I have my stuff up there. My bedroom. Nobody should be up there!"

Skipper began running up the stairs to the balcony. Vicky chased after him, demanding that he stop.

But he didn't stop. He was in the balcony now, and he saw Mallorie.

"Ohhhh," he groaned. "She's dead!" He turned toward Vicky and said, "You killed somebody! You're bad!"

Mallorie tried to thrash around to show him she was still alive.

"Uh-oh," Skipper said. He got a pocketknife from his pocket and cut Mallorie free as Vicky fled the theater, taking off in her white Subaru.

"Thank you," Mallorie wept when she pulled the gag off. "Thank you!" Only hours before, she had recoiled from the man in disgust. Now she threw her arms around him, hugging him and thanking him over and over.

Skipper kept saying, "Oh boy, oh boy,

oh boy." Then he looked hard at Mallorie and said, "You got change for coffee?"

....

Word got around quickly about what had happened. The police arrested Vicky at her house and charged her with attempted murder. She confessed to everything—even to creeping around Mallorie's house the night Mallorie thought Skipper had followed her home.

Amazingly, *The Werewolf of Warwick* opened on schedule, and both Brendon and Mallorie as well as the rest of the cast got good reviews. But the townspeople were convinced there was a bad omen of some sort lurking in the theater. Not many people came, and the play closed after one weekend. Even though she felt bad for Mr. Axton, who decided to find a new theater somewhere else, Mallorie was relieved. She wished Brendon luck but told him she didn't want to see him anymore.

Brendon didn't seem heartbroken, nor was Mallorie surprised by his reaction.

During the trial, Mallorie had to testify about everything that Vicky had done to her in the last few weeks. She asked the court to order Vicky to seek mental help, rather than put her in jail. Mallorie really believed that Vicky was a decent person. She just had to be set straight again.

Vicky was ordered to get mental health treatment. Her parents chose an institution in another state. They sold their house and moved to be closer to her. Mallorie never had to see Vicky again, and that was fine with her.

....

On a warm October afternoon, about two weeks after the trial ended, Cole and Mallorie were eating tacos at a jazz festival. The events of the last few weeks had drawn them closer together. Cole had really been there for Mallorie during the trial, and she was beginning to see him a little differently than she had before.

"Skipper likes that little room we found for him," Cole said. "It's close to my mom's bakery, and after what he did for you, she promised him a free, fresh donut every morning with his coffee."

"That's cool," Mallorie said. She smiled

at Cole. What was so different about him? Was he taller? More muscular? Did he comb his hair a different way? "And so are you, Cole."

Cole grinned shyly, and then it struck Mallorie. She knew why, all of a sudden, she found him so appealing. It was not that he had changed—she had. She realized now that good looks and charm could not replace someone who would stand by her through thick and thin as Cole had. She had not been willing to give him a chance before.

But now she was.